Mrs V Beveridge

Lilac Peabody

and

Bella Bright

Also by Annie Dalton:

Lilac Peabody and Sam Sparks

The *Angels Unlimited* series:

Winging It
Losing the Plot
Flying High
Calling the Shots
Fogging Over
Fighting Fit
Making Waves
Budding Star

Lilac Peabody

and Bella Bright

ANNIE DALTON

Illustrated by Griff

An imprint of HarperCollinsPublishers

First published in Great Britain by HarperCollins*Children'sBooks* in 2004
HarperCollins*Children'sBooks* is an imprint of HarperCollins*Publishers* Ltd
77-85 Fulham Palace Road, Hammersmith, London W6 8JB

The HarperCollins*Children'sBooks* website address is
www.harpercollinschildrensbooks.co.uk

1 3 5 7 9 8 6 4 2

ISBN 0 00 713772 9

Printed and bound in England by
Clays Ltd, St Ives plc

1. The Amazing Vanishing Girl

This story starts when I'm three years old. I'm sitting on my dad's knee, sucking a lolly, watching Mama and Auntie Louisa flying through the air like angels. At least, Dad said it was Mama and

Auntie Louisa. They were so high up, they could have been two springy little dolls in sparkly leotards.

"That'll be you one day, Bella," Dad whispers. "Won't that be wonderful!"

I drop my lolly in the dirt and burst into tears. My parents actually expect me to *fly*! I'm only three years old, but I already know that performing on a trapeze is not my idea of fun.

Fast-forward six years. I'm nine and a half years old and I'd love to tell you my fear of heights has gone away. But it's got worse. Over the years, that first baby fear has become an icy terror of absolutely ANY situation where I have to perform in public.

A wimpy circus kid! Can you *imagine* the shame?

I'm desperate. My fear problem is too big to solve by myself, but there's no one I can turn to. I can't tell my parents because they're part of the problem. I can't tell the other circus kids because they're *real* circus kids. Every chance they get, they're walking around on their hands or balancing on tightropes – while I skulk in our trailer reading like a geek.

I can't even tell Sam, my one friend at school, because he's *not* a circus kid, and he just wouldn't understand.

That's why magic is my only hope. In fact, you could say that wishing is like my full-time occupation. Every time I blow out my birthday candles, or find a wishbone in my stew, each

time I see a shooting star zoom to earth, I screw up my eyes and silently beam my wish to wherever wishes go.

PLEASE make me not be scared of heights.

I believe in magic, I do. There's just one small problem. I don't totally believe it can happen to me. Perhaps that's because I'm not a very

noticeable kind of kid. I don't fit in, but I don't stand out, either. When I'm with the other circus kids, I feel like a boring little moth in a crowd of gorgeous butterflies. At school, I'm simply too weird to bother with. Some of the local kids don't like circus people. When they think the teachers aren't looking, they call me bad names, like "crusty" or "dirty tink". But most kids just look through me like I'm not there. Sometimes I feel like the Amazing Vanishing Girl.

So I'm doing all this frantic wishing, but deep down I'm afraid it's hopeless. The truth is, I'm not sure the Universe will actually take any notice.

Then, one night, it does...

It's the last day of October. My Auntie Lou throws a big Halloween party for the kids on the site. I'm no good at parties, but it will look weird if I don't go, so I make myself a pointy cone out of black card (witch's hat), wrap a piece of old blanket around my shoulders (cloak) and trudge across the site to Auntie Lou's trailer.

Dad has gone to visit Mama in the hospital. Later he comes to find me. He chuckles when he sees me surrounded by rowdy vampires and skeletons. "Its good to see her having fun," he tells my aunt.

I feel like an evil double agent, because I'm secretly longing to go back to our trailer so I can finish my book.

Back home, I take my book and myself off to bed. Dad comes in to say good night. "Not long now," he says. "Soon have your mama home."

After he's gone, I try to sleep. A new moon is glinting through the gap in my curtains, exactly the shape of someone's fingernail. There's a clatter outside, one of the dogs knocking over a bin. I peek at my clock. Ten minutes to midnight.

I keep remembering Honey's taunts at home time. "No one likes you, Bella Bright," she taunted. "Sam only puts up with you because he's new. He'll drop you the first chance he gets."

It's just my luck that the one kid who notices me is the class bully. The trouble is, Honey's right. I'm a freak. I don't fit in anywhere.

I slip out of bed, pad across to my dressing table, and open a drawer. Inside is a small squishy parcel. Taking a deep breath, I unwrap the creased and crumpled paper and lift out a pair of small, narrow slippers of kitten-soft leather.

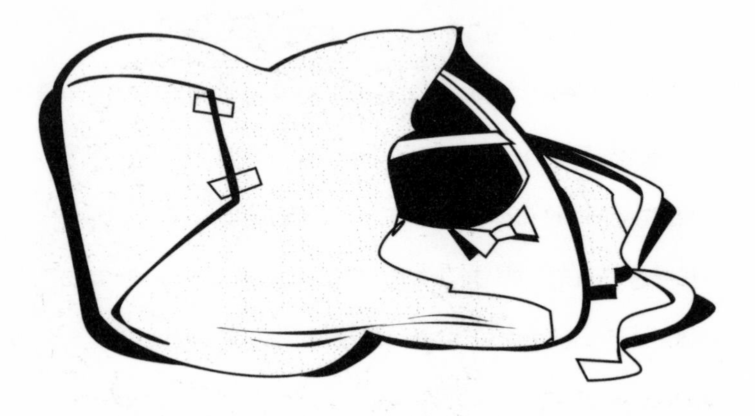

They are tattered and the original rose colour has faded. The soles are so worn they feel greasy to the touch. The slippers belonged to my great-great-grandmother, Bella Verdi, a famous trapeze artist at the start of the twentieth century. Mama gave them to me the day she went into hospital.

"All performers get stage fright at first," she said comfortingly, "but we all get over it. After this baby's born, we'll work on the trapeze every day. You're going to love it, I know."

Dad put his arms round us both and suddenly we were all crying. My parents were crying because they were scared something might go wrong with the baby. I was crying because my mother has this big dream that I'll grow up to be as talented and famous as Bella Verdi. Suppose I never get over my fears? She's going to be so disappointed.

Mama says the trapeze is in our blood. Her aunts, cousins and sisters are all successful trapeze artists. My twin cousins, Ruby and Sapphire, have NO problem with heights. It's so unfair. Why is the trapeze in their blood and not in mine? Why did I have to be the freak?

CRASH! Another bin goes over. What's got into the dogs tonight? They're charging all over the site like puppies. Maybe they're spooked because it's Halloween.

My eyes go wide in the mirror. I quickly check the clock. It says twelve o'clock exactly. Dead on midnight. I snatch a glance at the window. New moon. Excitement whooshes through my veins.

A new moon at *midnight*, on Halloween! I've been so busy feeling sorry for myself, I almost let this triple-wish opportunity go by!

Luckily I still have one sparkler left from the party. I tiptoe into the sitting room and find the matches. Dad's snoozing in front of the TV. He never sleeps in his bed nowadays; he wants to be ready in case the hospital calls him in the middle of the night.

I creep stealthily past my sleeping dad. He lets out a juicy snore and I freeze, but eventually I make it to the front door.

Outside the frost makes each grass blade look like it's been dipped in silver. A baby is crying in Auntie Lou's trailer. My little cousin Emerald is cutting a new tooth.

One of the dogs comes up to be petted.

"Ssh," I shiver, "I'm busy."

I stare up at the night sky and the roots of my hair start to tingle. New moons mean new beginnings; my Italian granny told me that.

I'm suddenly dizzy with excitement. I'm taking action! Tonight I'm going to make the Universe

sit up and notice Bella Bright!

Before the feeling fades, I light my sparkler and recite, "I wish I wasn't scared. I wish I was brave like Bella Verdi."

I feel a funny little "click" inside my chest.

Someone heard me!

I drop my sparkler in a panic, leaving it spluttering on the grass. I bolt indoors, hurtling past my snoring dad and into my room.

Diving into bed, I pull the quilt up over my head.

There's a soft fizzing sound. I can see a strange starry light sparkling through my covers, as if my sparkler has followed me indoors. I've been wishing for magic since I was three years old. But now it's really happening I'm too scared to look!

I huddle in the dark, trying not to make a sound, which is hard because my teeth are chattering violently.

"Hmm," says a voice. "Not ready, eh? OK, we'll try again tomorrow."

The sparkle effect fades.

It was a dream, I tell myself, trembling. I've been tucked up in bed all the time. I didn't really make a midnight wish under the moon. It was just a dream.

Most kids get a lie-in on Saturday mornings. My twin cousins and I are up, dressed, and frantically squeezing between parked vans and trucks, taking the shortest possible route across the frosty field.

"If we're late, Uncle Boris will blow his top," pants Ruby.

We're sprinting now, hopping over coils of electric cable, dodging under clotheslines, our breath making white clouds as we run.

I can hear engines humming, bacon frying, voices joking, or squabbling, in any one of five different languages. No matter where I hear them, these sounds always mean home.

My parents and I used to be on the road with Bright's Circus fifty weeks a year. We'd drive our trucks to a new town, set up on a piece of waste ground, and do two shows a day for a week. Late Saturday night, after the final performance, we'd take down the big top, drive on to another town and do the whole thing all over again.

Then Mama found out she was expecting a baby. There was a problem, I don't know what, and the doctors advised her to stay in hospital until the baby was born. Dad couldn't bear to leave Mama in a strange town all by herself. He called a meeting and told everyone they had to find a new ringmaster. "We'll catch up with you just as soon as we can," he explained.

But that isn't what happened! When Dad and I moved on to this site, everyone in the circus came too! Show people aren't perfect, but in a crisis we stick together.

To help pay the bills, the adults started a circus school. Now every Saturday, my cousins and I mix buckets full of coloured "gunk" for trainee clowns to throw over each other.

"Uh-oh," Saffie mutters, "Uncle B. doesn't look happy."

He isn't our real uncle, but we've grown up with Uncle Boris, so he's like family – not very nice family. "I never thought a clown would be such a mean old grouch," Sam complained when he met him.

Uncle Boris never seems to feel the cold. It's freezing and he's just wearing a string vest with baggy old tracksuit bottoms. "You're late!" he snaps.

"By about sixty seconds," objects Saffie.

"Try jumping from a trapeze when your partner is sixty seconds late." Uncle Boris unlocks the van and shoos us inside. "Twelve buckets," he growls. "Full to the top, mind."

"How come they never make the boys do this?" Ruby moans after he's gone.

Saffie laughs. "Because they'd have an all-out gunk fight!"

My cousins chat while they work. I envy Saffie and Ruby. They're sparkly and fun like circus girls are supposed to be.

And they don't have a scared bone in their bodies.

"So how's it going at school?" Saffie asks me.

"OK," I say cautiously.

"Have they stopped picking on you?"

"Oh, you know..." I say awkwardly.

"Bella!" Saffie scolds. "These people will stomp all over you if you let them."

"We're going into town after," Ruby says. "Want to come?"

I shake my head. "We're going to visit Mama."

We finally emerge from the gunk van. I head back to our trailer. I hate it when my hands are all gunky and I'm desperate to wash.

A split second before I reach the door, something makes me look up. A small flock of birds has settled on our roof.

How weird, I think. I've never seen them do that before.

Next minute, the birds take off. For a moment the air is full of fluttering wings, then they're gone. Just one bird has stayed behind.

A shiver goes down my back. It's not a bird.

A strange shimmery little creature is smiling down at me, just as if we're old friends.

"Hi Bella," she says. "I'm Lilac Peabody."

2.
A Shining River of Wishes

She's not a bird, she's not an animal, and she's definitely not human – she's too small. Also her skin is the wrong colour, and her eyes are too big and wise. Plus she has this weird kind of glow.

My voice squeaks with fright. "How did you know my name?"

"Oh, names are the easy part of my job," she says airily.

Lilac Peabody has weird hair, too, in springy little bunches. Her clothes look as if she's borrowed them from a fairy's fancy-dress box.

I try to imagine what "job" this weird little creature could do.

"Are you... an angel?" I ask uncertainly.

"An angel called Peabody?" she grins. "Nah! Doesn't have the right ring!"

I glance around nervously. A magic creature is sitting on our van in full view. Amazingly, no one seems to notice.

"But – but what are you?" I stutter.

Lilac unexpectedly spreads a pair of teeny wings and flutters down to join me.

"Think of me as an extraterrestrial busybody," she says calmly. "You *were* wanting the full magic makeover, weren't you?"

I swallow nervously. "I don't – I don't think I know what that is."

"Oh, magic makeovers are great fun," she beams. "Don't worry, I promise not to turn you into a frog."

I hastily back away. "Could you really do that?"

"Never tried," she says cheerfully. "Shall we go for a walk? People are wondering why you're talking to yourself!"

We walk down to the canal. Well, I walk. Lilac Peabody flits happily beside me, like a strange shimmery little bird.

I must be really slow on the uptake, but suddenly it dawns on me why she's here.

"You were in my room!" I gasp.

"Correct," Lilac agrees.

"Because of my wish?"

"Also correct," she says.

I stop in my tracks. "HOW? How did you know? How could you possibly know to be listening at that exact moment?"

"I'm a professional wish consultant, didn't I say?" she says coolly. "We have certain Powers."

I hear a whizz of tyres and just manage to jump out of the way as a boy zooms past on his bike. "Dirty crusty!" he yells over his shoulder.

Lilac watches him pedal away. "Does that happen often?"

I nod unhappily. "Saffie says they're idiots and not to take any notice."

"Hmm," says Lilac. "I prefer a more direct approach."

She purses her lips and blows. There's a clunk and a muffled yell. The boy and his bike go in opposite directions. The bike falls into the canal with a splash. The boy topples into a large nettle patch.

I'm shocked. Lilac Peabody just made a kid crash his bike. Because of me.

The boy staggers out of the nettles, whimpering with pain. He sees me hovering. "YOU did that," he says accusingly.

I can't explain what gets into me then.

"Yeah, I did," I tell him angrily. "I knocked you off your bike and if you call me names again I'll put a hex on you!" And I make a scary gesture.

I see him change colour. Suddenly he goes streaking away up the towpath. As I watch him hurtle into the distance, I feel as if I'm coming out of a dream.

I just threatened a complete stranger. Me! Mousy Bella Bright!

Lilac chuckles. "Nice work, Bella. He'll think twice next time."

But I just feel ashamed. People in this town call us bad things as it is. Now that boy thinks I put some gypsy curse on him.

"I don't see how it helps, making someone scared of me," I say stiffly. "That boy could have gone in the canal, you know. He could have drowned."

She sounds huffy. "Hey, I was *aiming* for the nettles, OK. Besides, he needs to learn a little respect."

"I'd better go," I say abruptly. "We've got to visit my mum."

We're not going for ages, but suddenly I feel really wobbly. I need to get away so I can think.

"OK, Bella, catch you later," she says calmly.

I feel a hopeful twinge. "Really? You're coming back?"

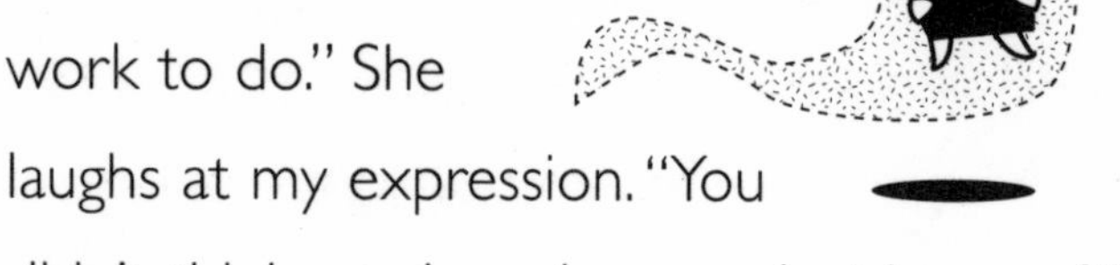

"I told you," she beams. "We've got work to do." She laughs at my expression. "You didn't think magic makeovers just happen?"

On the way back to our trailer, I'm in a daze. The Universe has finally noticed me – big time! Not only has it noticed me, it's sent Lilac Peabody, highly trained wish consultant and magic makeover artist, to sort me out.

"Oh wow," I whisper shakily. "Oh WOW!"

When we get back from the hospital, Dad checks the phone messages. "Sam wants to know if you'll go ice-skating tomorrow."

"Oh," I say. "I can't. I'm – I've got this uh, thing for school."

Sam's my best mate, but he's a boy, and he wouldn't understand about magic. Right now, magic is all I can think about.

Tonight or maybe tomorrow, Lilac Peabody will use her Powers to take away my fears, and I can start training to be the next Bella Verdi. I hardly dare to believe it, but it looks like I'll actually get to live happily ever after!

I wait in my room all evening.

When it gets to five minutes past midnight, I know she's not coming.

You can't blame her, I think miserably. *She did offer, but you're like, 'Oh, no! I've got to go away and think.' You had your opportunity and you blew it.*

I still don't want to believe it's over, so I force myself to stay awake. But I'm shattered from two late nights, not to mention my massively weird day.

My eyelids keep closing, and suddenly I'm having my bad dream; the one I have almost every night...

I'm trembling on a wobbly platform high above the circus ring. Down below, the upturned faces of the crowd look like pale little dots.

I hear a sudden drum roll. Next minute Mama and Auntie Louisa come zooming through the air towards me on a swing. They're so happy that I'm finally going to perform with them; they're beaming all over their faces. Suddenly they flip upside down, holding their hands outstretched. "Jump, Bella," Mama smiles. "We'll catch you, don't worry. Just do it like we practised."

But I just freeze.

"I can't," I whimper. "I'm sorry Mama, I just can't do it..."

I wake up with tears running down my face.

My room is filled with a soft starry glow. A tiny figure is perched beside me. "Hush," she says. "It was just a dream."

I wipe my eyes. "Why did I have to be called Bella Bright?" I choke out. "Bella means beautiful, did you know that? What a joke."

"It's a wonderful name," says Lilac warmly.

"For somebody else. Not me." I swallow. "Honey calls me Mouse Girl."

In the silvery starlight of my room, Lilac Peabody's eyes shine like a friendly cat's. "Tell me how you and Honey fell out," she suggests.

I feel my face get hot. Not even Sam knows the truth. The fact is, Honey has every reason to hate me.

Lilac just waits.

I give a shuddery sigh. "It's hard to make friends when you're on the road. So, even though I was worried about Mama, I was pleased when Dad said we'd have to stay put for a while. At first, my new school was just like all the others, everyone calling me a dirty crusty, but one day this girl stuck up for me."

"Honey," nods Lilac.

"I did notice the other kids seemed scared of her, but Honey was always sweet to me. It turned out she'd always dreamed of joining the circus. She wanted to be a juggler.

"Auntie Fran is a brilliant juggler, so I asked if she'd teach us both. Honey was thrilled. She said I was her best friend."

I swallow. "We started spending all our weekends at the circus school. Some nights she'd come by after school and Dad would let her stay for tea. Honey said my dad was a good cook." My voice trails off.

"So what happened?" asks Lilac.

"Every month the students at the circus school put on a display to show everyone what they've learned. Honey and I had been working hard on our routine. Auntie Fran said we were ready to perform in public. Honey kept saying, 'I can't believe my dream is coming true.' I should have told her I couldn't do it, but she was my friend. I didn't want to let her down."

"Of course you didn't," says Lilac softly.

I shudder. "When I ran on, and saw all the people watching, I went all cold and clammy. My heart was thumping so hard, I truly thought I was going to die. I couldn't even see straight. I blundered into the table that was holding our juggling kit. It collapsed like a joke table.

Everything went flying. Honey stood there in shock. I just ran out. Can you believe that? I left Honey all by herself."

I have to blow my nose. "Afterwards, I tried to explain but she just stormed home. Maybe she thought I did it on purpose."

"You must have felt horrible," says Lilac.

"That was the good part," I say bitterly. "I'd seen Honey being unkind to other kids, but she'd never said a mean word to me. But after that, she went all out to make my life miserable. She told everyone in our class that circus people eat dog food and we never wash and that our trailer smells. No one would sit anywhere near me."

I have to stop again for another blow. "Then Sam came to our school, and he had this mad

Afro. Honey started calling him Poodle Head. I know how it feels to have Honey on your case, so I plucked up the courage to talk to him, and after that we became friends."

Lilac gives me a searching look. "Have you told Sam how you feel?"

"No way! Then he'd despise me, like everyone else."

"If he's your friend, he won't go off you because of one little thing," she points out.

"You don't understand. Being scared has ruined my life. I've been wishing and wishing to be brave," I choke, "but I'm still scared."

Lilac sighs. "Bella, I've never met any child who wished so hard as you. If you were able to see all the thousands of wishes you've wished over the years, you'd see a shining river of wishes streaming into the Universe."

"Really?" I whisper. "You can see wishes?"

"But they never came true did they? Didn't you ever wonder why?"

I feel myself go red. "I was doing it wrong, wasn't I? I should have used thee and thou, and lots of big words."

Lilac shakes her head. "It's not HOW you wish that's the problem."

I stare at her and I get a horrible sinking feeling.

"It's the wrong wish," she explains. "And if it's the wrong wish, no matter how hard someone wishes, it can never ever come true."

3.
The Sparkle Training Programme

I cry so hard, my eyelids puff up like popcorn.

"How can it be the wrong wish?" I sob. "I only wanted my life to stop being scary. Is that so wrong?"

"Yes. You think if you weren't scared of heights, your life would be happy. But if you were happy inside, you wouldn't let your fears get you down. At the moment you go around as if your life is just a big bad dream, which makes it almost impossible for the Universe to grant your true wishes."

"My life IS a big bad dream," I wail. "You're being SO mean, Lilac Peabody! You've got these amazing Powers and you won't even do this one little thing."

She just pats my pillow. "You should get some sleep. We're starting your training programme tomorrow."

I sit bolt upright. "What kind of training?"

I'm talking to the air. Lilac Peabody has just vanished like a soap bubble. Did I just imagine the whole thing?

No way, I think. If I was going to imagine an extraterrestrial busybody, I definitely wouldn't give her weird little bunches. And she absolutely would not criticise me for making the wrong kind of wish.

Next morning, Sam leaves a string of messages. I don't call back.

When it's time to visit Mama, I tell Dad I've got a stomach ache. If I go, she'll start talking about trapeze lessons, and I'll just fall to pieces.

After Dad drives away, I just sit on the step of the trailer staring at nothing. *What's the point of magic,* I think. *It just makes things worse.*

Auntie Lou is sitting on her step too, gently bumping noses with baby Emerald to make her chuckle. "No hospital today?" she calls.

I mime having tummy ache. My aunt goes back to bumping noses with Emerald.

People go dotty over you when you're a baby, cooing over your cute little dimples, but it isn't you they're seeing. They're seeing some perfect future child who's going to grow up to discover a new planet or invent a cancer cure and make them proud.

That's my deepest fear: that one day Mama will realise what a wimp I am, and have to pretend she doesn't mind.

There's a cool fizzing sound, and Lilac Peabody appears in a starry whoosh of light.

"Oh," I say. "It's you."

"I saw four Halloween pumpkins outside your aunt's trailer the other night," she says, as if this is a normal way to start a conversation. "Run and fetch one, please."

I stare at her. "Why on earth do you want a pumpkin?"

She grins. "So you can go to the ball, Cinder-Bella!"

We actually spend the afternoon making pumpkin pie. It takes all afternoon because I have to keep running to Auntie Lou for ingredients. You'd think you'd just need a pumpkin, wouldn't you? But you need eggs, raisins, sugar, the rind and juice of an orange, nutmeg and cinnamon...

On my third trip, my aunt comments, "Feeling better, I see."

"A tiny bit better," I say in a weak voice.

Finally the pie is in the oven. The smell of baking makes the trailer smell homey for the first time in weeks.

Lilac claps her hands like a teacher. "Let's make a start. Don't look so worried," she laughs. "This is the fun part. This is the bit where you get your magic makeover." Her eyes have gone wise and luminous.

Last night I wanted Lilac Peabody to magic my troubles away, now I'm not sure. "I d-don't really..." I stutter.

"Of course you don't," she beams. "That's where my unique training programme comes in." Lilac places a tiny shimmery hand over mine.

"You want to learn to sparkle, don't you? You want to shine?"

Her hand feels fizzy; not uncomfortable, but definitely weird.

"I don't think I know how," I tell her wistfully.

"Oh, I think you do, Bella," she says with a sly smile. "I'm afraid I played a trick on you. You see, we've already started."

I'm bewildered. "When?"

"About twenty minutes ago," she says breezily. "Don't you feel better for baking that pie? Your S.L.s improved almost instantly."

I stare at her.

"It's short for Sparkle Level," she explains. "Yours was alarmingly low. I've seen happier goats, actually."

I gawp at her. "Happy goats?"

She giggles. "Oops, I meant 'ghosts' obviously." Her expression turns serious, "You do know you were in danger of turning completely invisible?"

I feel a funny twinge. I've never heard of Sparkle Levels, but what Lilac Peabody says makes a weird kind of sense. "Are you saying people don't see me because I'm sad?" I say huskily.

"Yes, but don't worry," she beams. "You see, it's physically impossible to sparkle and be invisible at the same time."

Lilac tells me to check on the pie, then we do what she calls "Sparkle-cises". "They're called Sparkle-cises," she explains breezily, "because they're exerCISES that make you sparkle!"

After my first few Sparkle-cises, I start to wonder if this is some joke. Lilac makes me do some seriously silly things, like seeing how many crackers I can cram into my mouth at once, or singing "Sheep Black Baa Baa" while hopping on one leg. ("Baa Baa Black Sheep" backwards, if you're wondering.)

To make things more surreal, each time I complete a task Lilac produces a helium-filled blue balloon, apparently from thin air.

Finally I have to put a pair of knickers on my head (clean ones, obviously!) and walk up and down without laughing.

Well, by this time I'm laughing so much I can't stand up! Nor can Lilac. She is now holding so many balloons, she keeps being lifted off her tiny shimmery feet.

"Sorry, Lilac!" I gasp. "I messed that up."

"No, it was perfect!" she crows.

She shows me my reflection in the mirror. I look like a different person. My cheeks are flushed. My eyes are shining.

"I'm sparkling," I whisper.

"Yes, you are," she says softly. "You're actually sparkling!"

The oven pinger goes. The pie is ready.

"Well done, Bella, you've successfully completed the first lesson in the Sparkle Training Programme," she beams.

She solemnly gives me a balloon. "And remember," she says with a straight face, "when life hands you a balloon, try not to pop it."

I watch in amazement as the bobbing blue balloons carry Lilac up through the ceiling and out of sight. I run outside and stare up at the sky, but there's no sign of her anywhere.

I feel too fizzy from my Sparkle Lessons to stay home by myself, so I go down to the circus school. I wander past trainee jugglers and fire-eaters, proudly practising their new skills.

The clown students are perfecting a crazy gangster routine with a collapsing getaway car. I LOVE clowns. I think I get it from my dad. Before he became a ringmaster, he did this brilliant act with Uncle Boris.

A wild fantasy plops into my head, of a girl in clown make-up and baggy trousers emptying a huge bucket of gunk over someone's head! The wildest part is that I know this girl really well. In fact, she's me!

"Are you nuts, Bella?" I giggle. "Girl clowns don't exist. They probably don't even exist on Lilac Peabody's planet."

That evening I'm still in a great mood, so I phone Sam.

"Whoop-de-doo!" he says in a grumpy voice. "Thought you'd died."

"Sorry, it's been a bit hectic," I say truthfully. "Look, tell your mum not to pack you a big lunch tomorrow."

"Why?" he asks curiously.

"Just because, Mr Nosy!" I giggle. "OK, because I'm bringing a surprise pudding!"

"Yay!" says Sam greedily. "Now you're talking."

On Monday night, Dad goes to visit Mama as usual.

I'm just washing up from tea, when Lilac Peabody shows up for our next Sparkle Lesson. I tell her about my crazy fantasy of being a girl clown.

"You could do it," she says seriously.

"Yeah, right," I grin. "And for my encore I'll climb Mount Everest in flippers!"

She chuckles. "How was school?"

I swallow. "Kind of weird."

Lilac raises an eyebrow.

"Charlie Chase sat next to me at lunch time. I mean, he's only the coolest boy in our class! He LOVED your pie, by the way!"

"Well, it is an excellent recipe," she says smugly.

"Then I put up my hand in class, and Miss Mays actually saw me!" I have to swallow again. "Plus she started asking me all these questions about the circus. She said she's always wanted to do a circus project, so Charlie said, 'Then why don't you?'"

"What did she say?"

"She's told us to go away in small groups to think up some ideas. I'm with Sam and Charlie. I really wish Charlie had kept his mouth shut."

"Who did Honey pal up with?" Lilac asks curiously.

"She didn't. She said the circus was just for losers."

"She's still angry?"

I pull a face. "Still mean, anyway. She heard Dad saying goodbye to me so she started making fun of his accent in front of everybody."

Lilac puts her head on one side like a bird. "Did anyone laugh?"

"No," I realise in surprise. "Actually, they didn't."

"So, let's get down to work," Lilac says, clapping her hands.

Halfway through our lesson, Dad comes back, so we have to go off to my room.

I don't feel comfortable doing noisy exercises with Dad around, so Lilac says I can do some drawing. "Design the silliest dress you can think of," she grins.

I chew my felt tip for a while, then draw a cartoon girl in a disgustingly frilly party dress. I add corkscrew curls and put an enormous floppy bow in her hair. "Is that silly enough for you?" I giggle.

Lilac has a glint in her eye. "What about frilly socks?"

"Ooh yeth," I lisp, giggling. "Thweet ickle white ankle thocks."

"Good work, Bella," Lilac smiles. "You've got the costume and your character! You can help Sam and Charlie plan their costumes this weekend."

"Costumes?" I say nervously.

"You want to start work on your routine, don't you."

I just stare blankly.

"For the circus project," she explains. "You wanted to be a clown, now here's your chance!"

I stare at her. "That was just a daydream, Lilac. I'm not going to make a fool of myself in front of the whole class in real life, no way!"

"This won't be like last time," she insists.

"You don't know that," I wail. "You're not even from this galaxy, OK! You have NO idea what it's like to be a scared human child."

Lilac folds her arms, and her eyes narrow into slits. "Stop it, Bella! Life just handed you a beautiful blue balloon, don't pop it."

I surprise myself by bursting out laughing. "How cool are you, Lilac? You're rapping!" I start dancing around. "Hey, STOP it! When life hands you a balloon, don't POP it. Keep a grip and don't you DROP it."

She shakes her head admiringly. "You can't stop sparkling now, can you? Even when you're scared." She fixes me with her huge eyes. "Tell the truth, wouldn't you love to do a clown act with Sam and Charlie?"

It's true. The new Bella is desperate to sparkle and shine. But the old invisible Bella knows this would just end in tears. On the other hand, she hates to disappoint people. Lilac has put a lot of time and effort into sorting me out. It would be ungrateful of me to let her down after all her hard work.

"OK!" I say with my brightest smile. "It can't kill me, right?"

"It'll be wonderful," Lilac reassures me.

"Oh, yeah," I fib. "I know."

4.
The Bully and the Mouse Girl

"Fetch a doctor, I'm dying!" groans Charlie.

"I've got serious sugar shock!" Sam whimpers.

Baking chocolate brownies to take to our Saturday planning meeting was Lilac Peabody's idea. She said they'd break the ice. But since I arrived, the boys have done nothing but stuff their faces. Now they're rolling around on Sam's mum's carpet, clutching their bellies.

"Does anyone want to share their ideas?" I suggest timidly.

They don't seem to hear.

You're vanishing again, Bella, I think.

"You tell your ideas first," I repeat, more firmly.

"Too full," clowns Charlie.

"Me too," agrees Sam.

I swallow. "OK, I'll tell mine, shall I? I've been thinking about this, and I think Charlie should play the straight-man parts."

Charlie recovers in a flash. "That's just dumb," he objects, sitting up. "Everyone knows I'm the joker."

"Exactly! Everyone expects you to kid around. The more serious you are, Charlie, the more they'll laugh."

He cheers up. "You think?"

"She's right, you know," says Sam.

"You should play a really gormless character, a total no-brain," I tell him. "You can walk like this, look." I jump up and show Sam how he should move. Both boys fall about laughing.

"So who do you play?" Sam asks.

I giggle. "A really soppy, disgustingly sweet little girl."

"I LIKE it," Charlie grins.

What with hospital visits and practising clown routines, my life is getting hectic, but Lilac refuses to let me off my Sparkle-cises.

"You're doing so well," she says firmly. "You can't stop now."

One night we go back to Sam's house to try on our costumes.

Sam is going to be wearing a clown version of a boy's school uniform. Charlie has a suit, a top hat, and a bow tie.

"Where's yours?" Charlie asks.

I produce the hideous frilly dress Auntie Lou and I adapted from a frock we found in a charity shop.

"Don't you think it'th thweet?" I lisp coyly. "It'th my betht party dweth."

We put on our costumes and show Sam's mum some of our act. "You guys have worked so hard on this," she says admiringly. "You're going to wow everyone."

"How's school?" Lilac Peabody asks later that evening.

"School's OK," I say truthfully. "I think maybe these Sparkle Lessons are working."

It's true. Apart from Honey, everyone is really friendly to me these days. Kids are constantly asking me for tips on juggling and trampolining, or whatever their group is doing for the final show. The headmaster is so impressed, he wants us to perform in front of the whole school.

So far I've been able to blank this alarming thought from my mind.

Sometimes I kid myself I'm actually going to pull it off.

Then the big day arrives. Even before I open my eyes, cold panic hits the pit of my stomach, the icy terror I feel in my trapeze dream.

I totter to the bathroom to brush my teeth, but the toothbrush slithers weakly from my hand. "I can't," I tell the pale, wild-eyed girl in the mirror. "I'll faint, or I'll throw up on myself. I just can't, OK?"

I hate to let Sam and Charlie down after all their hard work, but it's better than humiliating them in public.

I phone Sam and stammer out some excuse about a stomach bug.

"Well if you're ill, you're ill," he says bravely. "Shame, your routine was brilliant. We'd have knocked their socks off."

I find Dad and tell him I'm sick. I look so terrible, he believes me. I fritter the morning away watching TV.

The phone rings around midday. Eventually I pick up.

"Sam? You sound all muffled."

"I'm whispering, you nutcase!" he hisses. "I'm using the office phone. I don't suppose you're feeling any better?"

"Not really, no," I say in a feeble voice.

"Bums!" he moans. "Honey's telling everyone you're just faking. She says she knew you wouldn't show. She says you were going to perform with her one time, and you totally dropped her in the poo. I wanted to prove her wrong, that's all."

I carefully replace the phone in its cradle. I pick up a cushion and hug it tight. "Where are you, Lilac Peabody?" I whimper. "I screwed up again, and I don't know what to do."

No one comes.

She's probably wishing she'd let me go totally invisible, I think viciously. I would, if I were her.

I stand up and pull a hideous face at myself in the mirror.

I look closer. What's that? It isn't a tear.

Am I imagining it, or is there the teeniest sparkle in my eyes?

I gasp. It's like Lilac said. I'm scared, but I'm still sparkling! Lilac Peabody's training programme actually worked!!

I rush into my room and start throwing on clothes. I grab my curly wig and costume and sprint out the door. If Dad gives me a lift, I'll just make it.

Unfortunately I can't find my dad anywhere. I rush over to Auntie Lou's trailer but she's gone out with the baby.

I stare frantically around the site. There's no one around. I'm about to give up, when I hear tinny music coming from Uncle Boris's trailer. I bang on his door so hard, I hurt my knuckles.

He comes out scowling, and listens to my garbled story. "You want to do what?" he growls.

We make it to the school seconds before the whistle goes. I jump out of the car and storm through the gate.

I can't see her in the playground, so I bellow at the top of my voice. "Come here, Honey Hope! I want to talk to you!"

The playground falls silent. Children nervously move aside. Finally, we're face to face, the Bully and the Mouse Girl.

"Thought I'd wimp out, didn't you?" I tell her.

Honey gives an evil laugh. "I *knew* you'd wimp out. You still will, Mouse Girl. You'll mess up – like last time!"

"Maybe I will wimp out," I say calmly. "And maybe I won't. You'll never know unless you come and see the show."

I stalk off to the hall to get changed.

Sam and Charlie come racing after me. Their eyes are like saucers.

"So are we doing it now?" Sam asks, confused.

"Yeah, we're doing it," I grin.

"Result!" He punches the air.

Half an hour later, Sam and I are in the wings, watching Charlie Chase on the stage playing a circus ringmaster, in his shiny black suit and bow tie. He bawls through a megaphone:

"We PROUDLY present the 'BRIGHT SPARKS'. Give them a hand, PLEASE, ladies and GENTLEMEN!"

Everyone claps enthusiastically.

Sam grins at me. "Putting our names together was such a cool idea," he whispers.

"Quick! You're on!" I tell him.

Sam runs on wearing short baggy trousers and an old-fashioned boy's blazer, and playing with a yo-yo. Looking completely gormless,

he tries to do all these stunts, but the yo-yo keeps surprising him by making mad noises. (It's really one of the boys doing sound effects!)

I sidle on in my hideous dress, my little frilly socks and shiny shoes, and my big soppy pink bow. I'm pretending to lick a large Ping-Pong bat, painted to look like a huge lollipop. I coyly offer Sam a lick. Sam goes all shy, and the whole school howls with laughter.

Our act goes like clockwork. Everybody adores the big pie fight where I accidentally "kill" Sam with a cream pie, and he falls over: splat!

I stuff Sam's "corpse" on to an old go-cart and wheel him to the undertaker, played by Charlie. He puts on a pair of joke spectacles and peers closely at Sam. Suddenly he delves into Sam's tummy and, with no expression, starts pulling out strings and strings of sausages.

This is the high point of our act. Unfortunately, a mobile phone goes off in the middle. The man quickly goes out to answer the call. I'm astonished to recognise Uncle Boris. I can't believe he stayed to watch the show!

He waits until we're taking our bows, then he hurries up the steps to the stage and grabs my arm. "We've got to go to the hospital," he insists.

My heart turns over. "Is it Mama?" I gasp. "Is she OK?"

"She's fine," he reassures me. "They're both fine."

I stare at him.

"Congratulations, Bella, you've got a healthy baby sister." And for the first time since I can remember, Uncle Boris smiles.

I don't see Lilac Peabody again until my sister is almost six weeks old.

Then one afternoon, Mama asks me to mind the baby while she pops to Auntie Lou's to borrow some tea bags. If you ask me she's just desperate to get away from my little sister's screams!

I lift the screaming, red-faced baby out of her crib and walk her up and down. But no matter what I do, she just yells louder. Then, for no reason, she stops. Her eyes grow wide, and she starts cooing lovingly at someone behind my left shoulder.

I spin round to see Lilac Peabody perched cross-legged on the sofa. "Hi Bella," she says calmly. "That's a cute baby."

"Yeah?" I grin. "You can have her if you like. She's been screaming since Mama brought her home. Mama says it's colic... I've missed you," I say shyly.

"I missed you too. Loved 'Bright Sparks', by the way."

"You were there?"

"You don't think I'd miss your big day! I was sitting next to your uncle. He was so proud."

I'm amazed. "Really?"

"Really!"

"So, would you say I, erm, sparkled?" I ask her shyly.

"No, Bella, I would say you *scintillated*."

"That's almost as good as sparkling, right?" I ask nervously.

"It's better! You can be very proud of yourself, Bella."

I have to look away, I'm so pleased.

"I told Mama, you know," I say abruptly.

"You told her you didn't want to perform on the trapeze?"

"She was totally cool about it."

"That must be a relief," says Lilac.

I sigh. "You'd think so, but you know what parents are like. Now they're all overexcited about me being the first girl clown! I said, 'Look, I'm nine. I don't know what I'm going to be yet. I might not want to work in a circus. I might be the first circus-kid prime minister!'"

I put the baby down…

she instantly starts whimpering again. Lilac leans over and plants a tiny kiss on my sister's tummy. The kiss turns into pretty sparkles which melt into her babygro. My baby sister stops crying, and gazes solemnly into Lilac's eyes, then she starts peacefully sucking her thumb.

"Wish Consultant, Magic Makeover Artist, Baby Charmer," I say admiringly. You can do all these amazing things, Lilac – you're like my fairy godsister or something!"

Lilac chuckles. "That's nice, Bella. I like that name."

"But I don't know anything about you," I say wistfully. "Like, where you go when you're not with me? Are you making some other kid dance around with her knickers on her head?"

"Hey, didn't you listen?" she laughs. "That was a unique training programme especially designed for the one and only, scintillating Bella Bright!"

"But have you even got a home, or a family?"

Lilac Peabody gives me a mysterious smile. "The Universe is my home. And I have all the family I need."

I can tell Lilac has really come to say goodbye, so I desperately try to keep her talking. "The baby hasn't got a name yet. Actually, I've very nearly convinced my parents to call her Lilac."

"I'd be honoured," she says softly.

"How is my S.L. looking?" I ask in a hopeful voice. "Maybe I should do some more Sparkle-cises to be on the safe side?"

She shakes her head, smiling. "Your Sparkle Level is absolutely perfect." Her eyes twinkle. "But if you ever start

turning invisible again, give me a call, OK?"

And she's just gone. No whoosh of starlight, no blue balloons. Just gone.

"That was Lilac Peabody," I tell my little sister huskily. "Sorry you didn't get to know her. She did say she'll come back if we ever need her."

I hear funny little grunting sounds. My little sister is snoring!

Maybe it wasn't colic after all. Maybe our baby was just waiting until someone finally decided on a name, because, for the first time in days, six-week-old Lilac is peacefully asleep.

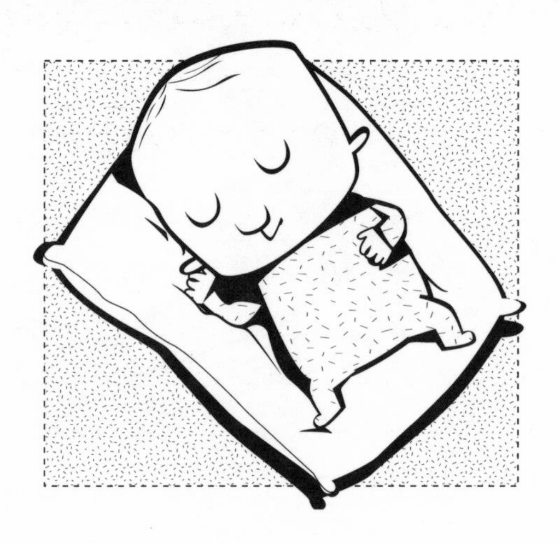

Sam hates moving. He's always having to start at new schools and make brand new friends… and then leave again. This time he's hoping to stay for good – but will he want to once he meets the school bully, Honey Hope?

ISBN 0-00-713771-0

Charlie Chase is the most popular boy in school. Always joking and laughing, nobody knows he has a deep, dark secret. Everyone wishes they could be like Charlie, but would they still if they ever found out… This could be Lilac's toughest challenge yet.

ISBN 0-00-713773-7

ANNIE DALTON ILLUSTRATED BY GRIFF

Honey Hope is a bully. She teases and taunts, sniggers and sneers. But why is she so mean? Will she even let Lilac Peabody be her friend...?

ISBN 0-00-713774-5

Witch-in-Training

Maeve Friel

Illustrated by Nathan Reed

Meet Jessica, Witch-in-Training!

On her tenth birthday, Jessica discovers she's a witch! But magic powers don't just happen overnight. With the help of Miss Strega, legendary witch trainer, she must practise the skills that all good witches need… and learn from disastrous, and often funny, mistakes along the way!

Magic and flying, goblins and dragons – they're all in a night's work for a witch-in-training.